The Devil Is in the Detail
and other writings

World Writing in French
A Winthrop-King Institute Series

There is a growing interest among Anglophone readers in literature in translation, including contemporary writing in French in its richness and diversity. The aim of this new series is to publish cutting-edge contemporary French-language fiction, travel writing, essays and other prose works translated for an English-speaking audience. Works selected will reflect the diversity, dynamism, originality, and relevance of new and recent writing in French from across the archipelagoes – literal and figurative – of the French-speaking world. The series will function as a vital reference point in the area of contemporary French-language prose in English translation. It will draw on the expertise of its editors and advisory board to seek out and make available for English-language readers a broad range of exciting new work originally published in French. This series is published in partnership with the Winthrop-King Institute, Florida State University.

Leïla Slimani

The Devil Is in the Detail and other writings

Translated by Helen Vassallo

Liverpool University Press

First published in English translation by Liverpool University Press 2023
Liverpool University Press
4 Cambridge Street
Liverpool
L69 7ZU

The Devil Is in the Detail was first published in French as *Le diable est dans les détails* (Éditions de l'aube, 2017)

On Writing was first published in French as *Comment j'écris* (Éditions de l'aube, 2018)

My Heroine: Simone Veil was first published in French as *Simone Veil, mon héroïne* (Éditions de l'aube, 2017)

British Library Cataloguing-in-Publication data
A British Library CIP record is available

ISBN 978-1-80207-884-8 hardback
ISBN 978-1-80207-885-5 paperback

Typeset by Carnegie Book Production, Lancaster

Contents

Introduction

"A shared story, full of humanity": Freedom and Commitment in Leïla Slimani's Writing

Leïla Slimani is a French-Moroccan writer and journalist. She was born and raised in Morocco to progressive Francophile parents who spoke only French with their children; at the age of 17 she moved to Paris for her studies and has lived there ever since. She worked as a journalist at *Jeune Afrique* for several years, and then moved to freelance work while she turned her attention to writing a novel. Her first attempt was not published (and, as she notes in *On Writing*, she kept the manuscript to serve as a reminder of what failure feels like), but after enrolling in a creative writing workshop run by the prestigious French publishing house Gallimard, an editor there saw the potential in her work. In 2017 Slimani was appointed Emmanuel Macron's personal representative to the Organisation Internationale de la Francophonie, a diplomatic role promoting francophone cultures, and in July 2022 she was announced as the chair of the 2023 International Booker Prize. These prestigious appointments indicate her key engagement with literature and culture both in France and beyond.

Slimani's first novel, *Dans le jardin de l'ogre* (published in English translation as *Adèle*),[1] was published by Gallimard in 2014. The story of a young woman's sexual obsession and rejection of bourgeois comfort and stereotypical femininity, it was well received critically and commercially. Slimani followed this with the psychological thriller

---

1   *Dans le jardin de l'ogre* (Éditions Gallimard, 2014). Translated into English by Sam Taylor as *Adèle* (Faber & Faber, 2019).

Chanson douce (*Lullaby*),[2] for which she was awarded France's most coveted literary prize, the Prix Goncourt, in 2016. This chilling story of a nanny murdering her young charges catapulted Slimani to international fame and remains her most celebrated title to date: in addition to the critical and commercial success of the novel, a film adaptation was released in 2019, as well as an adaptation for the iconic Comédie Française theatre.[3] More recently, Slimani has published *Dans le pays des autres* (*The Country of Others*) and *Regardez-nous danser*,[4] the first two books of a trilogy that fictionalises her family's past.

As well as these novels, Slimani has authored several essays and works of non-fiction: most notably, in 2017 she published *Sexe et mensonges: la vie sexuelle au Maroc* (*Sex and Lies: True Stories of Women's Intimate Lives in the Arab World*), which gives voice to Moroccan women caught between two ways of life.[5] In 2020 she was invited to write a lockdown journal for leading French newspaper *Le Monde*, and in the same year her essay "Our Mediterranean Mother" was published in the anthology *Europa28*, a collaboration between the Hay Festival and Wom@rt commissioned by activist publishing house Comma Press.[6] Though the majority of Slimani's writing is not autobiographical, it is inflected with her position as a young woman of North African origin, one who does not practise any religion and who rejects stereotypes of femininity. In her early fiction, Slimani inscribes herself into a literary heritage of writing Paris, and this connection with the city is echoed in her essays and short stories, whether in her solidarity with the French capital as it stands broken in the wake of terrorist attacks, or in the story

2 *Chanson douce* (Éditions Gallimard, 2016). Translated into English by Sam Taylor as *Lullaby* (Faber & Faber, 2018).

3 *Chanson douce*, film, directed by Lucie Borleteau (2019). *Chanson douce*, play, directed by Pauline Bayle (14 March–28 April 2019).

4 *Dans le pays des autres* (Éditions Gallimard, 2020). Translated into English by Sam Taylor as *The Country of Others* (Faber & Faber, 2021); *Regardez-nous danser* (Éditions Gallimard, 2022). Translated into English by Sam Taylor as *Watch Us Dance* (Faber & Faber, 2023).

5 *Sexe et mensonges: la vie sexuelle au Maroc* (Les Arènes, 2017), re-released in 2021 as *Sexe et mensonges: histoires vraies de la vie sexuelle des femmes au Maroc*. Translated into English by Sophie Lewis as *Sex and Lies: True Stories of Women's Intimate Lives in the Arab World* (Faber & Faber, 2020).

6 "Our Mediterranean Mother", translated by Sam Taylor. In *Europa28*, ed. Sophie Hughes and Sarah Cleave (Comma Press, 2020), pp. 67–71.

of a young girl transported through literature to Haussmann's nineteenth-century renovation of the city. There are also indications in both *The Devil Is in the Detail* and *On Writing* of the desire to delve deeper into her North African heritage and past, a desire that is borne out in *Dans le pays des autres* and *Regardez-nous danser.*[7]

The stories and essays that make up *The Devil Is in the Detail* first appeared in the French weekly newspaper *Le 1*, and were later published in France as a short volume in collaboration with Éditions de l'aube. The stories are reminiscent in style of Slimani's first two novels: they are written in short sentences, economical with words but extremely evocative. Many of the stories and essays deal with questions of Islam and fundamentalism, from a perspective that is determinedly Republican: writing in the aftermath of the 2015 Paris attacks, Slimani aligns herself very firmly not just with a mourning France but also with a secular one, a France that believes in freedom of speech and freedom of thought. In the fictional title story, she shows how terrorist attacks can be encouraged because people stand by and let the loudest or most hateful voices rise: in the essay "Our Gods and Our Homelands" she echoes this stance, advocating for tolerance, and for moving away from the global obsession with defining ourselves by our nationality and our religion. The essays represent a more sombre kind of writing than Slimani's fiction, often responding to tragic events in France's recent history. The raw pain and fierce indictment of the *Charlie Hebdo* attack in "An Army of Pens" underlines the tragedy of terrorism born of fundamentalism, and its reference to Salman Rushdie as an example of the freedom of speech and secular values that are so important to Slimani is particularly resonant given the attempt on Rushdie's life in August 2022. The final story in the collection, "Elsewhere", moves away from political engagement and towards Slimani's insistence on the social role of literature, focusing on a young girl who escapes the banality and solitude of her everyday life by reading, allowing books to take her on emotional journeys across the world.

On Writing is the transcript of an illuminating dialogue with Éric Fottorino, Slimani's commissioning editor at *Le 1*, that took

---

7 For a full list of Slimani's published work in French and English, see https://www.librairie-gallimard.com/listeliv.php?base=paper&mots _recherche=&auteurs=Le%C3%AFla%20Slimani.

place in the town hall of Paris's ninth *arrondissement* in 2017. In the course of the conversation, Fottorino and a live audience press Slimani on her writing approach and techniques, and the resulting text is an indispensable companion for readers and scholars wishing to become better acquainted with Slimani's œuvre. Though this is the transcript of a more spontaneous dialogue, Slimani nonetheless weighs her words carefully: Fottorino mentions how extraordinary the "density and depth" of her conversation is, as she offers thoughtful and considered responses that give significant insight into her writing practice and style. *On Writing* offers many keys to understanding her novels – both those published before it and those that have come since.

My Heroine: Simone Veil is a short essay on Veil, a feminist pioneer who was the first female president of the European Parliament and who fought for women's rights: the Veil law passed in 1975 legalised abortion in France. Yet Slimani also explores the restrictions Veil herself faced, from the publicly known traumas of her incarceration in Auschwitz during the Second World War to the more private constraints in her marriage to a man who, though she loved him deeply, could not accept her desire to be a lawyer. In *My Heroine* Slimani not only offers homage to Veil, but also writes of issues that still affect women today: she explicitly highlights the subject of women's sexual freedom in non-western countries (which she explores more closely in *Sex and Lies*), and it is particularly chilling to read *My Heroine* in the light of the overturning of Roe vs Wade in the USA in 2022. Slimani describes the restriction on women's bodies as archaic, indicating not only the regressive nature of such a decision, but also the fragility of women's rights. Like Veil herself, Slimani grapples with important and eternal issues of human rights and political intolerance, and is not afraid to face them head-on. The quotations from Veil that follow Slimani's essay offer timeless reflections on women's repression, as well as sobering reminders of Europe's role in contemporary society that are all the more piercing in light of the UK's divorce from the European Union and the war in Ukraine.[8]

The homage to Veil also intersects with the discussion of Simone de Beauvoir in *On Writing*, in which Slimani explores

---

8 These quotations also resonate with Slimani's essay "Our Mediterranean Mother" in *Europa28*.

the restrictions that women face because of social conditioning and expectations, showing how the question of women "having it all" is still as relevant today as it was in Beauvoir's time. These pioneers of recent history are of great importance to Slimani, and she sees women's emancipation as fundamentally linked to literature. Slimani believes that "a woman who reads is a woman who is emancipating herself", and affirms that having a "room of one's own" is important not just in the sense that Virginia Woolf intended when she first used the phrase – that is, having the time and opportunity to write – but also in the sense of having time and opportunity to read (a claim that takes on political resonance in Slimani's reflections on the levels of government-encouraged illiteracy in parts of the Arab world). These feminist sensibilities are echoed in Slimani's lockdown journal in *Le Monde* (one notable instalment of which was dedicated to women's confinement throughout history), further shaping the identifiable body of work that is so important to her.

Bringing these three pieces together in one volume for the translation creates a dialogue between them: from the conversation we better understand the stories, and through the homage to Simone Veil we see the depth of Slimani's engagement with women's rights. *On Writing* reveals many autobiographical details in Slimani's fictional work: discussing her love of reading, Slimani notes that as a child she found it difficult to distinguish between fiction and reality, and that even though her mother would repeatedly tell her to turn out her light and go to sleep, she would still carry on reading late into the night – experiences we see fictionalised through Rim in "Elsewhere". The importance of Russian and American literature is evident in Rim's experience and in the nourishment of her imagination (the topic that concludes the discussion in *On Writing*) and Slimani also reveals that – just like Rim – she first became acquainted with Paris through literature, poring over an old map of the city to bring to life the geography of the nineteenth-century French novels she was reading. There are also connections between the six stories and essays of *The Devil Is in the Detail*: for example, in the title story, Amine's daughter Mina is slapped by her teacher for the insolence of questioning whether a spider would have been able to spin a protective web across the entrance to the cave in which the Prophet Mohammed was hiding, and in "One Soldier, One Citizen" Slimani recalls this as an episode from her own childhood. Indeed, the essays offer many fruitful ways into deepening our reading of the short stories, particularly in their exploration of religion, secularism, intolerance and freedom of speech.

The style of the Russian authors Slimani so admires is evident in her work: she highlights Chekhov's ability to describe a character unequivocally in just a few sentences, a technique she practises successfully in her own fiction. The minor characters in particular come to life in the way they hold themselves and the way they interact (for a striking example of this we need look no further than Simone and Kader, the parents of the eponymous Adèle in Slimani's first published novel). Reading *On Writing* and then returning to "The Devil Is in the Detail" also shows some of the process behind this very tightly woven story in which much is left unsaid and yet every detail is extremely precise – a literary technique Slimani cites as having been influenced by Chekhov. Throughout her writing, Slimani's language shifts effortlessly between the elevated and the informal, but is rarely repetitive and always exquisitely constructed.

Fottorino ends his introduction to *On Writing* by describing Slimani's work as "a shared story, full of humanity", and this is key to her œuvre: whether it is in the exploration of marginalised characters in her early novels, the reimagining of her own family history in her more recent novels, the daily life of ordinary people in her short stories or the solidarity and engaged manifestoes of her non-fiction, Slimani writes of shared experiences and universal concerns, rendering her a writer whose voice resonates in many and varied contexts. Her commitment to writing, and to the importance of literature, awakens her curiosity to know what the future Leïla Slimani will find to write about, a curiosity that is no doubt shared by her readers. In "An Army of Pens", Slimani evokes the literary heritage of France as being intrinsically linked to Republican ideals of solidarity and freedom, shaping the France of today, and in *On Writing* she notes explicitly that she wishes to create a body of work that will inscribe her into this literary heritage: in so doing, she takes her place in the line of contemporary writers shaping the France of the future.

The Devil Is in the Detail

The Devil Is in the Detail

As he got older, Amine grew jittery. Amine Moussa, the university professor, loved and respected by everyone, is in the grip of anxiety attacks and insomnia. It makes his wife laugh. Atika jokes about his paranoia. She suspects it's a mid-life crisis because he's heading towards sixty. She doesn't understand him.

In the street, Amine is jumpy for no reason. He has started talking to himself. He feels ill at ease everywhere. At home, he can no longer stand being around the cleaner. He hates that old spinster, with her baleful look and her turned-down mouth. She proudly recounts how her brother left for Damascus and sends them money he's earned in the war. A lot of money. She raises her palms to heaven and thanks God for having guided her brother towards the jihad. A week ago, she warned Amine: "Mr Moussa, I can't carry on working for you if you drink alcohol. If I touch a bottle, God will forbid me entry into Paradise." He'd felt like asking her where she'd read such a stupid thing, but he hadn't dared. One evening, he caught her burning a match in front of his daughter. "You see, you and your parents, you're going to burn in the fires of hell, just like all the unbelievers who ignore the teachings of Islam". When he brought it up with Atika, she shrugged her shoulders: "Oh, let it go. She's a bit over-zealous, that's all. I don't know why you're getting so hung up on a detail. You're making too big a deal of it".

It's probably his age that makes the worrying worse. But he can't help picking up on every detail that ruins his day, stoking his unease and filling him with fear and shame. After dinner he gathers up the empty wine bottles, shoves them in rubbish bags and drives two kilometres to dump them in a bin. He's worried about being denounced by that red-haired guy who monitors the parking in his street, the one who's let his beard grow and calls the girls at the private school bitches and whores. "We should marry them off whether they like it or not, right professor?" Amine does not reply. Amine says nothing.

He keeps quiet when he gets in a taxi and the driver is listening to cassettes of a Saudi preacher. He hears him spit out his hatred of Jews and infidels and praise the fatwa that calls for the murder of all those who renounce Islam. Amine doesn't want any trouble. He pays for his ride and gets out.

Atika says he's blowing things out of proportion. That there are crazy people everywhere and that it doesn't mean anything. Admittedly she was furious when the teacher slapped their daughter Mina because she had dared to challenge a verse from the Qur'an: "I only said that it would have taken more than an hour for a spider to spin a web big enough to protect the cave where the Prophet hid out".

It was more than just a detail when a "brigade for the promotion of virtue and the prevention of vice" sprang up in the neighbourhood. "What do you make of that?" Amine shouted, waving a newspaper cutting under his wife's nose. These God-crazed people, armed with knives and sticks, attacked a group of youngsters and beat them to death. Because they went out at night, or because they didn't do their prayers or because they drank alcohol. No one really knows.

Amine has changed. The joy has gone out of him. He is obsessed with veils, those black nylon ramparts that have invaded the lecture theatres he teaches in, the beach he takes his daughter to, the cinemas where they cut even the most chaste kissing scenes. He wants to silence all the voices that have started raving about God, the devil, sharia law and the sacred honour of the women of this country.

He does not want to end up like his colleague Hamid, and bury his head in blissful nostalgia. He refuses to idealise the past, telling stories about the peaceful coexistence of Jewish neighbours, miniskirted girls and Marxist idealists on the faculty benches. He will not say that back then he never heard anyone talking about religion. Or that his father might well have done his daily prayers, but so discreetly that he doesn't remember ever seeing him kneel.

Atika is so sweet. Sometimes she manages to make him feel better, to help him see the beauty around him. She likes the festive atmosphere of the last days of Ramadan. And so to get her a treat he's made a detour this evening, to the El-Manar neighbourhood.

He goes to the Nour bakery to buy some of those stuffed crepes she loves so much and some candy for Mina.

People are queuing out into the street. They're jostling one another. They're getting impatient. A woman comes and stands behind Amine. He sees her walk up to the queue, her pretty face framed by a mauve veil. She stares at him. She shuffles closer to him. Gets so close that she's almost treading on his heels. "Maybe she's one of my students", he thinks. A young woman who comes to his classes but whom he can't quite place. Now he can almost feel her breasts against his back, her hot breath on the back of his neck. He must be imagining it. Such a beautiful young woman wouldn't be interested in him. She moves out of the queue. She is in front of him now, moving her face closer to his. He is just about to say something when she starts pointing at him and screaming: "He's been smoking! Him, here, he's been smoking! He's broken the fast, he smells of cigarettes!" A ripple goes through the crowd. From behind the till the baker calls out at her customers to calm down. Amine shrugs his shoulders helplessly. He takes a few steps back. Some men come towards him. They insult him, call on God as their witness. Someone pulls at his jacket. He runs.

An Army of Pens

19th January 2015

After the Toulouse attack carried out by Mohammed Merah in 2012, the literary supplement of *Le Monde* commissioned the writer Salim Bachi to imagine himself inside Merah's mind and write a piece of fiction. The result led to some very strong reactions. Some called it indecent; anonymous and intellectual readers cried out that it was "inappropriate", "disgusting", "scandalous" and "a moral outrage". A few days after the *Charlie Hebdo* massacre I was asked to do the same thing, and I took up the challenge. I genuinely wanted to give it a try, to get some sense of what could be going on in the minds of those young murderers. I did some research, I wrote a few lines. And I gave up. Not because I was afraid of what people would say. Not because I'm a coward or because I think that some subjects are taboo. But because I found it impossible to give myself over to an exercise like that, right at the time when France was going through such intense moments of emotion and reflection. If ever I am to write that story one day, it will have to be because of a deep need, an overwhelming urge to face that particular challenge.

Writers and critics will soon be expected to take a few steps back from this. To think objectively about it and weigh up everything that has happened. It is precisely because literature is an immense space of freedom, a place where anything can be said, where evil can be courted, horrors recounted, the rules of morality and decorum overstepped, that it is more necessary than ever. Literature brings complexity and ambiguity to a world that scorns such things. It can examine, openly and uncompromisingly, the ugliest things our society produces, the most vile and the most dangerous.

Literature carves out time in a world where everything moves quickly, where images and emotions triumph over analysis. But to make a real difference, literature has to live up to these ideals and its own standards. As Georges Bataille wrote, "Literature is everything or it is nothing. As a concept this does not indicate a lack of morality, but rather demands a 'hypermorality'".

Only a few days after the *Charlie Hebdo* massacre, Michel Houellebecq's *Submission* made all the headlines. Yet more evidence that France is a country where writers have an important role. Yet more evidence that literature is a space of free expression, whether or not you agree with the position the author takes. Houellebecq was called an anarchist, a sorcerer's apprentice and an Islamophobe, but also a genius and a visionary. He kindled an intense debate. One that begs the question: what responsibility does literature have? Should writers behave "responsibly" within the context of their country's geopolitical situation, or in the face of unrest? Should they censor themselves if they know that their work might inflame a society already on edge? I don't believe they should.

Should a man like Salman Rushdie be considered irresponsible? Of course not. Should Kamel Daoud, who also has a fatwa against him, be accused of pouring oil on the flames for having dared to say what he thinks about the direction Islam has taken? Obviously not. Is Alaa Al Aswany, the great Egyptian writer who has been physically attacked twice by the Muslim Brotherhood in Cairo, an anarchist? It is precisely because literature can say anything that writing it is so hard. It is precisely because literature does not fall back on over-simplified thought processes, generalisations or clichés, that it is important and essential.

Houellebecq might not be responsible, then, but he is honest. Though he is of course free to write whatever he wants, he is wrong to hide behind a false position of neutrality. He claims nonchalantly that no novel has ever changed the course of history. Maybe he's right. But I remain convinced that even if novels can't, readers can. Books might not change the world, but they can significantly shift the vision we have of it. They question it, clarify it, they call into question what humans know about the simple fact of existing in the world. During the massive demonstrations in France on 11th January 2015, how many people in the crowd and across the world were holding in their hand books by Voltaire, Victor Hugo, Emile

Zola, as if to acknowledge that those books also had their part in shaping the France we live in today?

When my first novel came out, I was weak enough to go and look at what was being said about it on social media. I was floored by the hateful messages that were being thrown at me from certain quarters, clearly those that uphold Islamist ideology. Beyond what I represent and what I write about, independently of the fact that in their eyes I am both a North African woman who has sold herself to the west and an infidel, for them my greatest crime was having written a novel. "There is only one book", they screamed in response. "Literature is just a way of glorifying lies". These fanatics, these uncivilised, ignorant barbarians only have one book to wave around, and they have misread it. Out of a population of 280 million in the Arab world, 60 million are illiterate. According to ALESCO (the Arab League's Educational, Cultural and Scientific Organisation), on average people in Arab countries only spend six minutes a year reading a book, and the vast majority of books published are about religion. All the Arab dictators know full well that if you educate people, you run the risk that they will overthrow you. That one day they will rise up, pen in hand.

Waiting for the Messi-ah

Up above Tangiers, in a place that looks out on both the ocean and the sea, lived a wise man by the name of Hamid. He was an old and pious man who had grown up fearing God and respecting his fellow men. Just like his father before him, every day he devoted himself with ardour and reverence to the five prayers. And when hard times started to befall him, when his wife died and he lost his job, it was in the Holy Qur'an that he found solace for his distress.

One evening when he was going back up the main street in the town, he heard some youngsters shouting from a café terrace: "Messi-yeah! Messi-yeah!" The old man was worried about the commotion, thinking that a fight was about to break out. In the crowd, he recognised his nephew Karim, a loud-mouthed deadbeat who had made this miserable little café his base. Standing up and waving his arms in the air, he looked possessed.

"What's going on?" Hamid asked him.

"Look, uncle", said Karim, pointing at a television standing on the counter. "Our new hero: Messi has scored a goal against Iran".

"Ah!" smiled Hamid.

He turned to go back on his way when his nephew took him by the shoulder and forced him to sit down:

"Doesn't that make you happy?"

"What does it have to do with me?" asked the old man.

"Anything that hurts those Shi'ite ayatollahs has everything to do with us. Don't you know all the harm the Shi'ites do to Islam? They're heretics and devil-worshippers. Don't you know that they spend their days insulting the Prophet's wife and the caliphs? On Ashura Day, while we're giving gifts to the children and celebrating with our families, they're whipping and stabbing themselves in the street until they bleed. Allah would never allow that. The Shi'ites aren't proper Muslims, and that's that. They don't know the true faith. And it makes me blush to tell you this, but they're also fornicators".

The old man's eyes widened.

"Oh yes they are!" his nephew continued. "Those dogs legalise marriages for a few hours so they can succumb to their twisted desires. Sometimes they swap wives with each other to give free rein to their fantasies. May God protect us from these heretics". Karim spat on the ground and went off towards the back of the room, where the youngsters were drinking beers on the quiet.

Hamid nodded his head, not sure what to believe. His nephew was prone to getting carried away and taken in by the most absurd rabble-rousing. He was just leaning on his cane to get up when the café owner came over to greet him. "Greetings, Si Hamid. Have you seen these youngsters? Worthless good-for-nothings. I heard what your nephew said, and he's wrong. He should not insult other Muslims in this way. Because Shi'ites are still Muslims: they pray facing Mecca and they worship our Prophet Mohammed, peace be upon him. Of course, they have strayed from the true path and have been manipulated by those crazy-eyed turban-wearers. But it is our duty to bring them back to the fold because we have the same enemy: Jews and the decadent west. America is dividing us, to better conquer us".

And he spat on the ground, as the old man looked on in disgust.

Hamid got up without a backward glance. As he went on his way he thought of his father, who used to teach in the local school and knew all the Sufi rites and the fables of old. His father had told him that in Persia, a country Hamid knew nothing about back then, men used to pray for the coming of a *mahdi*. "One day, at the end of time, justice will reign and despotic regimes will be abolished. Peace will be eternal and the wolf will lie down with the lamb. Women will never again be beaten or raped. On Earth, violence and poverty will disappear and all those who commit horrors in the name of religion will be punished. There will only be one religion and one humanity".

Was this dream an impious one? Had he sinned in wishing for the end of the world to be like this?

Hamid finally reached his front door, where his daughter Amina was waiting for him, looking worried.

"Where were you? It's very late".

She helped him to his room and served him a hot tea. She tried to make Hamid comfortable but he seemed distracted and preoccupied.

"What's wrong, father? What's on your mind?"

Sitting against the wall, his eyes half-closed, he told his daughter what he had heard. What the café owner had said, how angry Karim had been. "Ah", the old man said, scratching his chin. "What times we live in, my dear! If that's what modernity is, it doesn't do much for me. These days there are as many kinds of Muslim as there are makes of car. And each group thinks that they're better than the others. In my day, there was nothing like this. There were Jews, of course, and they were different from us. But we still celebrated feast days with them, didn't we? And we still said 'Sidna Moussa' out of respect for their prophet, didn't we? What times we live in".

One Soldier, One Citizen

18th November 2015

When I was a child, in Morocco, we learnt the Qur'an at school. Every day, part of the afternoon was devoted to reciting by heart passages from the Holy Book. To be completely honest, I've forgotten nearly all of it. I only remember a few litanies, but I don't even know what they mean. And I don't care. But I'll never forget the day when our teacher told us the story of the spider who, to protect Mohammed from his enemies, wove a web at the entrance to the cave where the Prophet was hiding. I was eight years old, the daughter of humanist parents who encouraged open discussion. I stood up and said: "But that's not possible! A spider couldn't do something like that, in such a short time".

The teacher came up to me. She slapped me, and said: "You should be ashamed to insult God and your prophet in this way".

When I got back home, I told my parents what had happened. I was sure they would comfort me, maybe even avenge me. They punished me. "You have to understand that sometimes you've got to keep quiet. Don't stir things up. You have the right to think whatever you like, but keep it to yourself. There's no point rationalising with people like that". My parents loved Voltaire and the Enlightenment, but I imagine they loved their children more. They were afraid. They were wrong.

After the terrible carnage that Paris has suffered, we are afraid to talk, afraid to write. The worst thing right now would be to say something stupid in a world that is already on its knees from ignorance and hate. To pontificate at a time when some are fighting for their lives and others are mourning their loved ones. So what should we write, then? If we have to use words, let's make sure they don't ring hollow. Because that too can kill: too much half-heartedness, too many compromises, too much cynicism. Our world, and in particular our world leaders, lack clarity, coherence, determination.

We have to acknowledge that acting on circumstances rather than principles does not protect us. Our moves are vain and pathetic, and our enemies laugh at them. They still want to annihilate us. If we're going to die, on a café terrace or at a concert, at least let us die standing up for what we believe in. I am neither a strategist nor an ideologist. I don't know how to fight such a threat. I don't have any solutions. We are all lost. But I am convinced that now more than ever we must believe in our way of life, in our freedom, and fight against the vile ideologies of these murderers. We owe it to those who, only yesterday, were killed.

I have only one thing to say to the barbarians, the terrorists, the extremists of all stripes: I hate you. We owe it to ourselves to be honest, to be dignified. To be truly French. We must stand up to our supposed allies from Saudi Arabia or Qatar, and to all those Muslim countries where every day more ground is gained by backward, conservative misogynists. Stand up to those who buy our weapons, sleep in the comfort of our palaces and are given public welcomes on the front steps of our institutions. How can we explain to our children that we are fighting against these barbarians when we ally ourselves with people who crucify their opponents and stone women to death? How can we explain to them that we are being killed because of our values of liberty, feminism and tolerance, of love for human life, when we are ourselves incapable of defending those values?

Let's stop hiding behind a pseudo-respect for other cultures, and a nauseating relativism that only thinly masks cowardice, cynicism and powerlessness. I was born Muslim, Moroccan and French, and I have this to say: sharia law makes me sick.

I have never been nationalist, or religious. I have always shied away from any kind of herd mentality. But Paris has been my homeland since the day I moved here. It is here that I became a free woman, it is here that I have loved, that I have been drunk, that I have known joy, that I discovered art, music, beauty. It is in Paris that I learnt how to live life to the full.

Victor Hugo once wrote: "Could such a city, such a capital, such a place of light, such a home to hearts, minds and souls, such a seat of universal thought, ever be violated, stormed, broken? By whom? By a savage invasion? It is not possible. It will never happen. Never, never, never! Paris will always be triumphant, but on one condition: that you, I, all of us here, be as one; together we will be one soldier, one citizen: one citizen to love Paris, one soldier to defend it".

Today, more than ever, I am conscious of how beautiful my city is. I would not exchange this city for any paradise of the kind the fanatics promise. Your fountains of milk and honey can't hold a candle to the Seine. I too will be that one soldier for Paris. Paris, which represents everything you despise. A delicious and sensual blend of languages, skins and religions. Paris, where couples kiss passionately on public benches, where at the back of any café you can hear families tearing themselves apart in political disagreement and then ending the evening toasting together to love. Tonight our theatres, our museums and our libraries are closed. But tomorrow they will open again, and it will be down to us – children of this country, unbelievers, infidels, wanderers, idolators, beer-drinkers, libertines, humanists – to write history.

Our Gods and Our Homelands

6ᵗʰ January 2016

I grew up in Morocco, I was born Muslim, and every year I celebrated Christmas in a big white house, in the countryside, between Meknes and Fez. All religions and generations were represented around the table. It was really quite something. Picture this: my uncle, a Jew, was a child during the Second World War and sought refuge in a village where members of the French Resistance protected him. My grandmother, who was from Alsace and spoke German, spent the war years in hiding in Switzerland. My grandfather, an Algerian Muslim, was an officer in the colonial army. But that evening, they would all share the same meal. It had nothing to do with religion, beliefs or nationality. My grandfather, who was very devout, didn't see any inconsistency in observing Ramadan and then dressing up as Father Christmas. Of course, we would argue sometimes. Some of them would get quite incensed. There were tears and raised voices. But we never left the table. We were together. Reunited.

This year, in Normandy, in the midst of the laughter and the conversations, I wondered what my generation would be capable of doing in this world. Will we measure up to those who fought so that they could celebrate Christmas together? Will we learn how to define ourselves by something other than our gods and our homelands? Will we always and forever have to prove our allegiance?

I am the child of all these foreigners, and I am French. I am an immigrant, a Parisian, a free woman, convinced that it is possible to be what we want to be without denying this possibility to others. That nationality is neither a glory nor a virtue. That there is joy in living in the here and now. That's what I would like the France of 2016 to be like: like those long and joyful Christmas meals, where everyone was welcome, where no one judged either the drunkenness of some or the outspokenness of others. Where the older generation did not dismiss the things the younger ones cared about, where everyone present chuckled at the blasphemers. Where at the end of the day the only thing that mattered was the awareness of how lucky we were to be together in a world where everything is hell-bent on dividing us.

Elsewhere

The afternoons always seemed interminable to her. Her father would take an afternoon nap and, because he was a light sleeper, he insisted on absolute silence. The lightest footstep or the quietest whisper would be enough to wake him. Rim knew this from experience. It had happened to her a couple of times and she had been punished, sent to her room until dinner. Her mother was never there in the afternoons. The cleaning ladies would be working at the laundry house. When Rim was little, they used to take her with them. They would lie her down on the damp sheets and let her fall asleep in the clouds of steam from the irons. But then she grew too big, too talkative, too unbiddable, and the women cast her out of their world. They told her to go and play elsewhere. To find something to do.

Rim couldn't leave the big house that her father had had built in a remote part of town, at the end of a deserted avenue. It was a cold and angular building, with huge glass windows instead of walls. The only people around were construction workers. They would fall asleep under the scaffolding, and Rim was scared of them. She never walked down that avenue. Nobody would have wanted to accompany her, and there was nothing to do there anyway. Besides, she had been told that young girls shouldn't walk around in the street.

Rim pressed her forehead against the windowpanes. She watched the hours go by, like an albatross locked up in a little cage. She wanted time to pass, and life to begin. She felt that something else was waiting for her. It was at that age, around thirteen or fourteen, that she began to travel. She had pushed her bed up against the window to make the most of the light coming in from the garden. She could hear the sound of the wind in the poplar leaves. She would sit down with her back against the wall and her legs stretched out, and the journey would begin. She went to Russia.

She walked along Nevsky Prospect on the arm of a poet dying of hunger. She slept in squalid apartments rented out by mean and hunchbacked landladies. She drank gallons of tea and vodka, ate raw onions and bitter cucumbers. She waited on Anichkov Bridge for someone who never showed up. She who had never seen the snow felt the frozen ground of a battlefield beneath her feet. One morning, under a violet sky, she took a boat along the Volga. She travelled by train, by car, on horseback. Before her was Love River. Rim was a convict, a pariah, an enemy of the people. Her limbs broken, her hands covered in chilblains, she carved out a path that no one had ever taken.

Sometimes life got mixed up with her dreams. "Dinner's ready!" "Coming!" "Get your head out of that book!" In the schoolyard, her classmates played their games. They didn't hear the screech of the locomotive, the shock of the crowd, the shrill voice of the little man selling kvass. They did not understand why Rim was so sad. Anna Karenina was dead and Rim was in mourning. She went around as if she were sleepwalking. Reality seemed dirty, banal, confused. Her soul was completely filled up with a strange languor, with feelings she had never before experienced and that she did not entirely understand, but that she felt acutely. Her joyless, tedious childhood, shaped by silence and repetition, had become populated by dreams. She had made friends who could never betray her and who never lied.

Her father did not have a job. She knew he was bored, that he was bitter, that life had no meaning for him. Every day he would sit in the same place on the red-and-white sofa whose arm was stained from his cigarette smoke. In front of him, on the table, on the floor, between the cushions, were piles of books that no one dared to touch. One day he held one out to her, the way that you would throw a ball to a dog. To keep her quiet, to make her go away. That day, she discovered America. From New York to California, she crossed the continent. She especially loved the sultry South, the magical name Alabama. Faulkner's Mississippi, Fitzgerald's Jazz Age. She saw the frontiers of the West come into focus. Her nostrils were filled with the dust kicked up by the horses' hooves. Every day, she came back to sit at her father's feet and he gave her his scraps. He gorged her with stories. He gave her New York and the plains of Montana, the shores of the Pacific, the heavy stillness of Albuquerque, the melancholy of rural Atlanta.

She would read as she walked along, as she sat in the car, at the back of a bus, in secret under a table, the book propped on her knees. Every night she turned the light back on, long after her mother had come to tuck her in. Every morning she looked pale and tired. They stared at the blue circles under her eyes that made her look older, as though she had already lived. "This child doesn't sleep properly. She's restless. It must be the books clouding her mind". In Paris, they were digging the *grands boulevards*. Rim drank glasses of beer on the banks of the Marne. A man, madly in love, had rented her a luxury apartment. She was a courtesan, an actress, an opera singer. Before long she was bloated from alcohol, and had pawned her last jewels. She had never seen Paris and yet its streets were familiar to her. She knew by heart the names of the boulevards, the yellow glow of the streetlamps, the frenzy of the Montmartre cabarets.

She had lovers from every corner of the globe, from Northern China to the heights of Bahia, from the Sahara to the English moors. Men swept her away to a bench in Cartagena, where the fragrance of mango trees mixed with the scent of love. She, who was afraid of everything – the dark, thunder, strangers – fought in wars and went on expeditions, she trekked through jungles and weathered storms. She did not fear either the fury of animals or the madness of men.

Later, much later, she took planes, she crossed borders. She touched skins that did not smell of ink. The world seemed to her at once familiar and exotic, full of memories and ghosts. Rim left the house with the huge windows, the deserted avenue and her father's silence. At society dinners, in bed beside her husband, in the alleys of cemeteries or in children's playparks, Rim speaks to ghosts. She seeks solace in their voices. She blocks out the reality that dislodges them, cuts them short or stifles them with chatter. In the afternoon, sometimes she leaves work and checks herself into a hotel room. No one knows she is there, sitting with her back against the wall. She stretches out her legs, she seeks out the sound of the wind in the poplars. And off she goes.

On Writing

Leïla Slimani in Conversation
with Éric Fottorino

Foreword

It's not often that a writer agrees to take part so generously and spontaneously in an exercise as invasive as delving deeply into how they write. And yet that is exactly what Leïla Slimani agreed to do in the dialogue that we have transcribed here in all its richness. No subject is off limits for the author of *Lullaby*, which won France's most prestigious literary prize, the Prix Goncourt, in 2016. She talks about her doubts, and her early struggles as a writer – all relative, of course, because her second novel earned her the highest possible accolade – or the pressures that come with the total and unmitigated commitment that writing requires.

In the course of our conversation, Slimani distils her advice and beliefs clearly and concisely, frequently returning to her position as a young North African woman who does not speak Classical Arabic. Her parents, Francophiles to the core, never passed it on to her ...

The density and depth of Slimani's conversation is striking, whether she's talking about Simone de Beauvoir or the writing workshops where she studied under her editor at Gallimard, Jean-Marie Laclavetine ("write about events, don't describe situations!"), or the status of women writers, which is uniquely challenging, even today, and especially for women writers who have children. The sections of this interview that focus on women's experience are particularly powerful, especially when Slimani states that a woman who reads is a woman who is emancipating herself.

As we listen to Leïla Slimani, we go on a journey through Russian literature – from Dostoyevsky to Chekhov – and American literature – Faulkner, Toni Morrison, Philip Roth. We hear a voice that is profound, authentic and sincere, convinced that even if literature doesn't exactly change the world, it can at least change those who write as well as those who read – and that itself is no mean feat. It is certainly enough to justify a life dedicated to the permanent pursuit of a "once upon a time" that leads you to explore worlds and souls through characters yet to be invented.

The Goncourt laureate says she is curious about what "the future Leïla Slimani" will want to write about later … In the meantime, the Leïla Slimani of the here and now gives us this gift: bringing us closer to the adventure of words, and the emotions and ideas they hold within them. An extremely valuable adventure, comprised as it is of fears and apprehension, vertigo, solitude overcome, so that at the end of the road a story rises up: a shared story, full of humanity.

Eric Fottorino
Director of the weekly newspaper *Le 1*

On Writing

Éric Fottorino: There is a long-standing relationship between Leïla Slimani and *Le 1*. She first wrote for us in 2014, two years before winning the Prix Goncourt. Every time Leïla submits a new short story or essay to us, the team is immediately struck by her writing, and her spontaneity. There is never a superfluous or ill-placed word. When you read her writing it seems very simple, but of course, as always with great writers, when it's simple it's actually complicated.

I looked at the archives and, Leïla, you are the twelfth woman to win the Prix Goncourt. The first was Elsa Triolet in 1944, for her novel *Le premier accroc coûte 200 francs* (Denoël).[1] Then there was Béatrix Beck with *Léon Morin, prêtre* (Gallimard, 1952)[2] and, of course, much later, Marguerite Duras with *L'Amant* (Minuit, 1992),[3] Edmonde Charles-Roux with *Oublier Palerme* (Grasset, 1966)[4] and then, more recently, Lydie Salvayre and Marie NDiaye.[5] Twelve women is still a small number, and looking at the quality of those works, you realise that when the jury have awarded the prize to a woman, more often than not they're honouring a great book. There are far more male winners, and so the quality of the books can leave something to be desired.

Lullaby is a Goncourt winner, but first and foremost it's a novel that hooks you instantly. When I read it, at the start of last summer, I was taken aback that this story had been written by a young woman, a wife and mother, with one young child and another on the way. Did your hand tremble when you wrote the first pages of that book? How was it that a young mother, pregnant with her second child, was able to plunge – and plunge her readers – into such a chilling universe?

---

1 Elsa Triolet, *A Fine of 200 Francs*, translated by Francis Golffing (Reynal and Hitchcock, 1947).
2 Béatrix Beck, *The Passionate Heart*, translated by Constantine Fitz Gibbon (Julian Messner, 1958).
3 Marguerite Duras, *The Lover*, translated by Barbara Bray (Harper Perennial, 1992).
4 Edmonde Charles-Roux, *To Forget Palermo*, translated by Helen Eustis (Weidenfeld & Nicholson, 1968).
5 Lydie Salvayre, *Pas pleurer* (Éditions du Seuil, 2014), translated into English by Ben Faccini as *Cry, Mother Spain* (MacLehose Press, 2016); Marie NDiaye, *Trois femmes puissantes* (Gallimard, 2009), translated into English by John Fletcher as *Three Strong Women* (MacLehose Press, 2012).

Leïla Slimani: I think there are two distinct kinds of fear as a writer, or at least for me. There is the fear of writing, by which I mean the fear of writing badly, of not pinning down my subject, of not getting my characters right. And so I do feel a kind of fear when I sit down at my desk, but not at all in terms of what I write. It's not the content that scares me; on the contrary, that's something that gives me freedom, an absolutely immense space of liberation. And when I sit down to work, I am no longer really me. I am no longer a woman, no longer Moroccan or French, I'm no longer even in Paris or anywhere else; I'm not bound by anything and so, ultimately, even my role as a mother doesn't come into play, I don't write as a mother. Rather, I'd say that I draw from my nightmares, from my deepest fears. I think that when you commit to writing, you have to commit completely. If there is any lesson I've learnt from writing my first two books (*Adèle* and *Lullaby*), it's that you can't do things by halves, or even by three quarters. You have to see things through and explore areas that might be unpleasant for you, and you also have to trust your reader. So many people have asked me whether I was afraid of scaring people, afraid that they would draw back and not want to read it, but no, I wasn't: I really do trust my reader. I've always liked what Toni Morrison used to say about her readers: she wanted readers who would engage with her writing, because she wanted to shake them up, to disturb them. I'm not trying to entertain, or to make sure my readers are sitting comfortably because, as a reader myself, that's not something I like. When I reach the end of a book, I like to feel almost uncomfortable, or at least unsettled. To have the sense that it has changed something. So that's what I try to aim for when I write.

Éric Fottorino: You definitely achieve that. If what I've read is correct, then the story of *Lullaby* was inspired by a news item, something that happened in Manhattan. Can you say more about that?

Leïla Slimani: The issue of inspiration is a complex one, too. For a long time I'd had this idea of writing about a nanny and working on the relationship between a mother, her children and their nanny. I found some old notebooks that date back to 2011 or 2012, and the idea for this story was gestating even then. But then, yes, one day I opened up a copy of *Paris Match* and saw some very shocking photos of a mother wrapped up in a foil survival blanket coming out of a building in New York's Upper East Side, surrounded by ambulances, and alongside the photos there was this terrible story of a nanny who one afternoon killed two children. The mother came home, she had her third child with her, and she found her other children's bodies in the bathroom. That story haunted me. Until that point I hadn't found my angle, I hadn't found my way in to writing this novel about a nanny. Because really the relationship between a nanny, children and a mother is extremely banal. Finding a narrative rhythm, figuring out how to make readers want to turn the page when what you're describing is a woman who turns up in an apartment, prepares the meals, changes the nappies, goes out to the local park, and then does the same thing the next day, and then the same thing all the days after that, a story that's ultimately very repetitive, is hard. That article about the murder was like a launch pad that allowed me to take off into fiction. But I don't go about it in the same way that Emmanuel Carrère and other authors do, where they work very closely with a news story, where their writing is a kind of investigation. For me, the news story was more of a trigger, something that gave me an idea, and from then on it's pure fiction.

Éric Fottorino: Did the fact that the real story happened in New York make it easier for you to fictionalise it by deciding to locate your story in the ninth arrondissement of Paris?

Leïla Slimani: Yes, setting the novel in Paris meant I had to build the story around particular places, and I couldn't have done that with New York. I needed it to unfold in the streets of Paris, and that made it more intense. *Adèle* was set in the ninth arrondissement, *Lullaby* takes place in the ninth and tenth arrondissements, places I know well. And it has a subject that interests me: gentrification, which is one of those big sociological words that nonetheless relate to visible everyday realities – such as the way in which women are treated in public spaces. These are things that interest me. How the city opens up – or doesn't – to women, mothers, children, pushchairs. They're the most ordinary issues, but when you try to weave that thread through the intrigue of a novel, you realise that they can be fascinating to discuss.

Eric Fottorino: Françoise Sagan used to say that she knew Paris better than any taxi driver – by which she meant that she could pinpoint any given street or side street. When you read *Lullaby*, it's impossible not to be struck by the meticulous way in which you depict rue Hauteville, the little park in Montholon Square, and so on. I imagine that you know those places so well that you don't need a map. Did you specifically want to firmly plant or root your story?

Leïla Slimani: I got to know Paris through literature. My first encounters with Paris happened through Balzac, Zola, Maupassant's *Bel-Ami* – the arrival in Paris – and of course *Les Misérables* and *The Hunchback of Notre Dame*. Back home in Rabat when I was a high school student there was no such thing as Google Maps – that would have helped me a lot – but my mother had some old maps of Paris. I used those maps to look up the streets the authors mentioned, I tried to understand what kinds of places they were, and Paris sprang up around me through literature. For me, the *grands boulevards* meant theatre cafés, the way they were in the nineteenth century. Parc Monceau was Zola's *The Kill*, where Renée has this extraordinary private mansion. Every district was linked to a book. So when I write about Paris myself, I want to become part of this lineage because I find it incredible that Paris is a city completely brought to life by novels. Paris is inhabited by Modiano, by all these people who have walked through her streets. I can never be in a Paris street without thinking of an author, a story, a setting, and so I want to write myself into that history. I know that readers – whether or not they're Parisian – respond particularly well to that.

Éric Fottorino: Let's come back to *Lullaby*. This is a story about a couple, a mother who wants to return to her work in a law firm, who enjoys going back to work but at the same time feels guilty for leaving her children. And then there's Louise, the perfect nanny who bends to every expectation – not just the parents' expectations but also the children's – or at least, so it seems. It's seamlessly written. One image stayed with me after reading – it's several months since I read it, so there are certain key things that I've retained – and it's the image of a chicken carcass. Could you strip the carcass for us now?

Leïla Slimani: That's the scene that traumatised my entire family. When they read the manuscript before the book was released, they said "seriously, how can you dream up such horrible things, we can't believe you wrote that". That chicken carcass ... you know, for me, that scene symbolises the kind of silent class conflict that plays out in this book. A lot of reviewers have mentioned the class conflict, and yes, there is a kind of class conflict, but it's not a conflict as such and it's not really about class. The conflict is always beneath the surface, there are never any raised voices, never any real arguments – in fact that's one of the problems with the relationships and it's exactly what fuels the misunderstanding. And there isn't really an issue of class, because the couple, Myriam and Paul, are modern professionals, slightly bohemian, who don't really consider themselves part of any social class. The nanny, on the other hand, has no social group so she has no security network: she doesn't think of herself as working class but she isn't middle class either, she's completely on her own. The two women have a very different relationship with food. Louise, the nanny, won't throw out anything: the tiniest scrap of chicken, a slice of ham past its best before date, a few peas ... she stores it all in plastic containers. Myriam and Paul find this both ridiculous and touching, and they rationalise it by saying that she doesn't have much money, she doesn't like to waste anything, and that at the end of the day she's in the right because they're wasteful consumerists. At first they reproach themselves for it and daren't say anything to her about it, but from time to time they rebel against it. One morning before Myriam goes to work she sees a roast chicken in the fridge that she thinks is past its best and so she decides to throw it out. She puts it in the bin. When she gets home at 10 p.m., tired from her day, the nanny is just behind the door. The moment Myriam opens the door, the nanny slips away. Myriam turns the kitchen light on and, on the kitchen table, sees a chicken carcass. She realises that it's the same one she had thrown in the bin, and that the nanny had retrieved it and made a meal for the children with it, feeling in some way personally insulted by her employer having thrown out a chicken that was still perfectly edible. Nothing is said, the two women don't dare confront one another or have it out, but that piece of meat – the leftover chicken that one of them can't bear to waste while the other prioritises her children's enjoyment, or well-being – comes to symbolise this silent conflict.

Éric Fottorino: The whole book is excellent, but that passage really stands out and I understand why your family asked you how you had come up with that, and what trauma they had inflicted on you for you to write such a scene! Without giving away the entire story, one thing that's really important, as it always is in any novel, is the mood, the atmosphere, and how the writing, the words you choose, contribute to that. You write in a very accessible way. Your novel isn't about concepts or grand ideas, it's storytelling pure and simple. It really comes alive, it's almost too real, both from the parents' perspective – it's not hard to guess what's driving the young woman – and from the children's. Can you say more about this? How did you manage to write the way the children see things, as finely if you were tuning a musical instrument? It's clear that they're very attached to Louise, but at the same time they're a bit afraid of her, because of the way she reacts sometimes.

Leïla Slimani: That was one of the hardest things about writing the book, one of the biggest possible pitfalls. Often in books or movies there is a tendency to make children too simple, to present them as very binary beings, very black-and-white, people who like or don't like something, who agree or don't agree with something. But I think that by a certain age, particularly the age of the little girl, Mila, children have very complex psychological relationships with others and are capable of understanding power relations, sometimes capable of manipulation. I don't mean that to sound negative or unkind, just that they can play one person off against another to get what they want. They also have a survival instinct, a kind of defence mechanism that helps them understand where they should position themselves, when they should be quiet and when they should speak. And on top of that, children don't necessarily seek out simple or clear relationships. They are often attracted to negative or mysterious people, people who might be quite dark, and that's how it is with this nanny who plays dangerous games with them – real games: there's always something at stake. The nanny isn't at all bothered about dumbing things down for them: she tells them very complex stories, plays very ambiguous and frightening games of hide-and-seek with them, but the children like it. Children like to be scared, and I was also trying to convey that, the kind of attraction – that as adults we forget – towards the dark side, witches, ogres.

Éric Fottorino: A little earlier you mentioned your first novel, *Adèle*, another fascinating text but with a different subject: *Adèle* is about obsession, and a young woman's sexual addiction. I recommend it to anyone who hasn't read it, it's another example of that uncompromising aspect of Leïla's writing: once you've started reading it, you're going to be drawn in right to the end, unable to skip a single word or page. The story will pull you in, and that's Leïla's great talent as a writer. Like with the nanny and the family and the children, she creates a universe that to all intents and purposes is quite banal, but it's precisely in that banality that something complex and gripping takes hold.

So let's talk about writing. Leïla, in your essay "An Army of Pens" you said that "Books might not change the world, but they can significantly shift the vision we have of it. They question it, clarify it, they call into question what humans know about the simple fact of existing in the world". Do you remember writing that? Can you tell us more about what inspired it?

Leïla Slimani: Like anyone who enjoys and takes an interest in literature, I have of course always asked myself that clichéd million-dollar question: what can literature do? I don't think that literature changes the world – these days we see the world cynically or realistically enough to realise that, unfortunately, that isn't going to happen. But I have myself experienced how literature can change me as a person, and I am very aware that if I hadn't been the reader that I am, I would not be the person that I am. Literature has played an enormous part in shaping my values, and in who I am as a citizen, as a woman. I know how carnal the relationship with literature can be, to the point that it can become a part of you, that it becomes an organ in its own right. I am convinced – and I'm speaking here as a Moroccan woman, and because I've seen it in my own country, just as in other Arab countries, countries where on average people spend only six minutes a year reading a book, where two hundred and eighty million people are illiterate, countries where for years reading has been forbidden because of policies implemented by dictators who have decided that people should not read because reading is dangerous, it can lead people to rise up against you – I am convinced, then, that reading makes us stronger citizens, and that reading as women makes us stronger women. I think that reading is very important for women across the world, because a woman who reads is a woman who is emancipating herself, setting herself free, giving herself time for herself – just like Virginia Woolf said. A room of one's own isn't only about writing books, but about reading them too. And still today, in many parts of the world, so many women just don't have the opportunity to be alone, to shut themselves away and take a moment to read. And those moments help us, I think, to truly become free citizens, they encourage us to develop a vision of the world that is liberated from what we're told to think, from common beliefs and popular opinions.

Éric Fottorino: You're obviously a great admirer of Russian literature, of Chekhov and the great Russian writers. Do you remember whether, as a child or an adolescent, there were particular books that – even if they didn't change your life – made you understand that literature could break down walls and open horizons?

Leïla Slimani: Absolutely. Russian literature especially. I still remember the first time I read Dostoyevsky. It left such an impression on me. I'll never forget my mother coming into my room and saying, "I'm warning you, if you haven't turned your light off by the next time I come in, there'll be trouble", and even then I still couldn't put it down. I remember reading *Crime and*

Punishment, and in particular the murder scene, which I think is one of the most beautiful murder scenes ever written. It's absolutely extraordinary, the madness Raskolnikov spirals into, and that exploration of evil, of madness, of the lack of morality means that in the end you stop caring about any moral judgement of him. That liberation, the possibility of moving away from the real world where we spend our days judging or having opinions, where people are on one side or the other – that liberation is extraordinary.

I've always loved literature from the south of the USA as well: Faulkner, Toni Morrison ... and, if we're talking about American writers, Philip Roth, too. I loved *The Human Stain* and *Patrimony*. In *Patrimony* Roth writes about his father's death: we're used to autofictional writing in France, and in a way *Patrimony* is an autofictional novel, but for me it brings something else to the table. He writes so unreservedly that it blew me away, and scared me, too, because it's so incredibly powerful. So Philip Roth had a great impact on me, too.

And then there are the Latin American authors, Mario Vargas Llosa, for example, and *The Feast of the Goat*. It's funny because when you've grown up in the Morocco of Hassan the Second, where an ageing dictator controls the media, and old spies sit in tatty raincoats on café terraces, and then you read *The Feast of the Goat*, which is about a similar situation thousands of miles away, you feel like you're in the same place, going through the same thing. Language builds a bridge, reading builds a bridge, and it's an incredible feeling.

Éric Fottorino: On the subject of language, could you talk a bit about French and Arabic? You write in French, do you write in Arabic?

Leïla Slimani: That's a big subject. I'll have to write about it someday. My parents were born in the '40s and they were both educated in French. My mother went to a convent school, and my father was one of the few indigenous people – as they were called at the time – to be accepted into French school. They were selected based on their intellectual ability – three or four Moroccan kids who were taught about "our ancestors, the Gauls" and so on, and who got a very good education. My father was from a very humble background. There were no books at home, and every day he walked past the house of a woman, a protestant widow, who gave him a whole library. She gave him many books, beautiful classics that I still have, I held onto some of them. So my father was a great Francophile, and loved French literature. My mother did, too. Then in the seventies, as young adults, they wanted a more modern Morocco, a more open Morocco, a Morocco where women weren't hidden away, where there would be gender equality and a much more secular Morocco than it is now – back then the word "secular" wasn't used, but religion was certainly less important there than it is now. My parents were very drawn to European and western culture. Back then it wasn't shameful to say it. Nowadays, when you say that you like western culture, it can create a terrible backlash. But because of their admiration of western culture my parents didn't think to pass on to us something very basic, and that was our language, Arabic. My parents always spoke to us in French. Of course we speak *darija*, the Arabic dialect that you hear in the streets, but they never raised us with Classical Arabic, the language that you read in the newspapers or hear on the news. It's one of my greatest regrets, and I often reproached my parents for it when we clashed during my teenage years. They were never really able to explain why they didn't pass it on to us, but it was the same for a whole generation in North Africa: all our countries have this issue with language that is both complex and fascinating.

Éric Fottorino: Let's look at a few photographs. Do you recognise this place?

Leïla Slimani: It's the Gallimard offices.

Éric Fottorino: The first time you went to the Gallimard offices ... I want you to tell this story because in the audience there are young people – or even not-so-young people – who want to write, who dream of writing, and who would like to get their writing published, or at least improve their technique. What was it that brought you to the Gallimard offices one day?

On Writing

Leïla Slimani: I had been working as a journalist for several years, and I had just left my post at the news magazine *Jeune Afrique*. I had a small child and I had decided to write a novel. I spent about a year on that novel, and I put my all into it – poured my heart and soul into it, as they say. It was the most important thing in the world to me. A friend of mine, a Moroccan writer called Abdellah Taïa, put me in touch with Louis Gardel, an editor at Éditions du Seuil. I gave him the book, and he told me that there was some good stuff in it, and that he'd take it to his editorial meeting. I spent two long weeks waiting anxiously for him to get back to me, and in the end I received an awkward and convoluted email in which he told me that it wasn't bad, but no better than that – not bad, but not good enough, and that it had a lot of flaws. I fell into a deep depression, my ego was crushed. My husband was very supportive, and said, "Don't let it break you, you can't let yourself wallow like this. It's to be expected that you didn't get anywhere with your first attempt, so you need to get back in the saddle and start again. I've seen that Gallimard run writing workshops, so why don't you sign up? If it goes well you might rediscover your love of writing, and it could be the push you need to help you move forward". To start with I wasn't entirely convinced, but then I thought, "why not?" And it turned out he was right. So the first time I went through the door of the Gallimard offices, it was to attend a writing workshop led by my current editor, Jean-Marie Laclavetine.

Éric Fottorino: So what clicked? What was it that made a disappointed young woman who'd been knocked for six, who wondered whether she had what it took to carry on, fall back in love with writing and come up with the opening chapters of *Adèle*?

Leïla Slimani: First of all, I think that for writing, as with any creative process, you need a combination of pride – because you have to have at least a little self-belief – and, more importantly, enormous humility. By that I mean the ability to accept when you've got it wrong, when what you've written isn't good, the ability to accept that this time it wasn't great or this time it didn't work, and as such to be open to how someone else responds to your text, to what you've written. When you're in a situation where you're the novice and someone else the expert – and for me that expert was Jean-Marie Laclavetine – ultimately it reinvigorates you, gives you your strength back, because you embraced that humility. Something new might open up, and at that point I had shut down, buried myself in this internal dialogue, where I was going round and round in circles. In France literary creation is too often seen as something almost innate, in the sense that you're born a writer or you're not, you're brilliant or you're not. There probably are such people, born writers destined for greatness, but I think there are a lot of people who just need to work hard, to meet the right person at the right time or need inspiration to strike at the right moment. Jean-Marie also gave me some simple tricks to help move my scenes forward, and it was as if lots of things that I already knew but hadn't managed to articulate suddenly had space to develop.

Éric Fottorino: Can you share one of those tricks with us?

Leïla Slimani: He gave me some very simple advice, for example the importance of being able to distinguish between a situation and an event in a novel. That's key. If you spend your time describing situations, the novel won't work because nothing's going to happen. You always have to be able to make clear what it is that you're writing about: am I writing about a situation, or am I developing events that move the story forward? Writing about situations is often quite easy, but writing events …

Another thing he said that has stayed with me was: "Don't get bogged down in explaining what your characters are thinking. Say what they're doing, and trust the reader to draw their own conclusions". I realised that, as a reader, I myself expect to be trusted, and so I have to be able to do the same with my own readers.

Éric Fottorino: That's very good advice from Jean-Marie Laclavetine. Continuing with the subject of creative inspiration, I remember the first time I called you on the phone. I asked you to write a text for my weekly newspaper, *Le 1*, and you said, "Would it be okay if I wrote a Chekhov-style short story?" What did you mean by that? It's certainly an excellent story, in the sense that everything is clearly expressed but at the same time much is left unsaid. It makes me think of what André Gide once said: "You know what you've written, but not everything you've written".

Leïla Slimani: Chekhov is one of my favourite authors, I regularly read and reread his stories. For me they're the best writing guide you could wish for, because he writes with such simplicity – or at least, he gives the impression of extreme simplicity. His writing is very clear, very pure, and goes straight to the point. His short stories are often around four or five pages long, and in those five pages he'll have sketched out an entire life, leaving you completely devastated. What fascinates me is his ability to capture a character in a couple of lines. He gives two or three details and you understand everything, he doesn't have to resort to psychological descriptions. Whether it's in the way a character holds their pipe, the way they walk, the way they talk to others, you know immediately what it means. And then Chekhov had a kind of narrative theory, a theory of fiction. He theorised that trademark simplicity, that restraint, by saying that if, for example, you write at the beginning of a chapter that there is a gun in the room, by the end of the chapter that gun must have served a purpose. You don't write for the sake of writing, you don't write a scene for no good reason, you're scattering a trail of crumbs and by the end it all has to lead somewhere.

When you called me, I asked if I could write a Chekhov-style short story, but in reality I was petrified, wondering what on earth to do. And then you said, "you can write whatever you like", which is the most terrifying thing in the world. Okay, I can write whatever I want, but what do I want to write? And so, of course, I went back to my first point of reference. That story was about Islam, and about conservatism. They're subjects that get so much airtime these days, but often from the same point of view. And I thought about how sometimes it's the little daily details that speak volumes, not the grand theoretical discourses. That's how the idea for the story came to me. A story about a person, just an ordinary character, a professor who's going to the bakery.

Éric Fottorino: That makes me think of Georges Simenon when he said: "If you want to say that it's raining in a novel, then write that it's raining".

Our next photograph is of Simone de Beauvoir, who won the Prix Goncourt in 1952 with the second volume of *The Mandarins* (Gallimard), a great novel about a group of French intellectuals which featured fictional representations of Albert Camus and Jean-Paul Sartre. Reading interviews with you and hearing you talk, I know that Simone de Beauvoir is very important to you. You said just now that to be a writer you have to work to become one. She said: "One is not born, but rather becomes a woman".

Leïla Slimani: Simone de Beauvoir has also written beautifully on the subject of women and literary creation. When I write, I always think of all those women, dead or alive, who have not had the chance to create anything, who were unable to write because of their situation, because of the simple fact of being women. And each time I write, each time I speak, each time I meet my readers, in a way I'm in mourning for all those women. Simone de Beauvoir asked how it was possible for women to create master-pieces when they aren't in a position to create at all. Whether or not they could have produced masterpieces we'll never know, because they just didn't have the chance to write them. Virginia Woolf said much the same thing. For a long time it was taken as given that women only existed to procreate. Women were immanence, and men transcendence. Women had their feet firmly planted on the ground, looking after the home, while men could aspire to greatness. Men have always been given the opportunity to create, to do great things. They could become divine creators, gods making their own universe. That was never an option for women. And on top of that, if they wanted to write, it meant turning their back on their home, their children, and also turning their back on the kind of modesty and discretion that is expected of women, because as soon as you start writing, as soon as you pick up that pen, as soon as you decide to get your work published, as a woman it's extremely subversive in terms of your social role, because you're consenting to lay yourself bare. Simone de Beauvoir has always deeply moved me in that respect: she theorised her decision not to have children. She didn't start a family because she wanted to be an intellectual. And right at the end of her life, in the last volume of her autobiography, *The Prime of Life*, she wrote about the doubts creeping in. She admitted that she wondered whether she had been right, whether it was natural or dreadful that she had made that choice and that she had been obliged to sacrifice being a mother in order to write, because women had been so conditioned to believe that if they wanted to create, in a certain way they had to become men. The judges of the Prix Goncourt used to say that there was no such thing as a great woman writer, and that if women were great writers then they were men. Obviously, I completely disagree with that point of view. Simone de Beauvoir wondered whether women could have it all. That's the question I engage with in my novel, too, in the end. Can women have it all, can they do everything? But even that question is a question framed by men. If we didn't have this ingrained assumption that women should be in charge of looking after children and household chores, we would never even ask the question of whether they can have it all, because we never ask whether men can have it all. To my mind, what's interesting with Simone de Beauvoir is that she totally changed the way of looking at it. She was absolutely right to say "one becomes a woman", because it's the world that makes us women. The street makes us women, taking the metro at night makes us women, coming up against a potential employer who asks us if we're thinking of having children any time soon makes us women. And so even if you don't want to, you become a woman, because society imposes it on you.

Éric Fottorino: In a very interesting interview you did for *Elle* magazine,[6] there is a passage in which you note that some of your friends reacted to your writing career by saying, "That's great, you'll be at home, so you'll be there to look after your son". And you replied: "No, I'm going to write, so my son will be in day care".

Leïla Slimani: That's such a typical response: "Oh wow, you're going to write!", meaning *she's so sweet, she'll write a couple of poems in her*

---

6 "Leïla Slimani, Superstar", *Elle*, 12 January 2017.

kitchen and then she'll go and pick up her son. "And it's so great because you'll get to spend time with him, that's so important when they're little". Well no, actually, I'm not going to spend time with him, I'm going to write. And then there are even moments when I could be with him, but I'll still get a nanny to look after him because I want to write. And as a writer it's awkward, because it's not as if you can say, "I'm off to the office, I'm off to the factory, I'm off to earn my crust and feed my child". There's a kind of selfishness involved that people don't want women to have. A selfish woman, one who claims for herself what she wants or needs, is a pariah. But I think that it should be normal for a woman to be a writer or an artist, whatever that might look like for her, and at the same time want to be a mother and not automatically be an unfit mother.

Éric Fottorino: Let's move on to the next photo. After the Gallimard offices and Simone de Beauvoir, here is al-Qarawiyyin University in Fez … tell us about this.

Leïla Slimani: Any Moroccan will tell you that al-Qarawiyyin is the oldest university in the world – but anyone from Bologna will tell you that's not the case. Let's not get into that debate, and just say that it's one of the oldest universities in the world. Even today it's still partially a madrasa with a mosque on the side, probably the most beautiful mosque in Morocco. Tradition says that it was founded by Fatima al-Fihriya, the daughter of a rich businessman from Kairouan, in the north of Tunisia, which is where the name al-Qarawiyyin comes from. It has a library full of extraordinary manuscripts. It's a great seat of learning, and is a true symbol of that medieval Islam founded on reading, on exegesis, an Islam that is open to the world, a welcoming Islam. The mosque still attracts many foreigners, especially from Africa and Indonesia, who come to do placements, to study in such a magnificent place. My father is from Fez, from that district.

A member of the audience: What happened to the "failed" manuscript that still had some good things in it? Did it end up as a drawer liner? Might you use it in the future? Will it be wasted, or can you salvage some of it?

Leïla Slimani: I've always thought that if ever I were to lead a writing workshop, I would bring it along, give it to my students and tell them: "this is a manual for what you mustn't do". When I don't know what to write, or don't know where I'm going with something, or think that what I'm writing is no good, I go back to that text, I read it and tell myself that's what "no good" really looks like, so it could be worse. I keep it beside me like a kind of literary scarecrow, but it will never see the light of day, or at least I hope it won't.

A member of the audience: How do you make yourself sit down and put pen to paper?

Leïla Slimani: There is always a very long gestation phase that you're not necessarily conscious of. For example, if we take the subject of my third novel, it's an idea I've had for a long time and that I return to often, but for the moment I'm not ready to write it. It's there, and I know I'll spend a few weeks digging deep and trying to get something for it out of everything I experience – in every conversation I have, and everything I see, I'll be trying to get inspiration for my novel. Then I'll lock myself up like a clam and shut myself away. At that point I'll be extremely focused, and that's when the writing will begin. What people often don't realise is the singlemindedness that writing requires. I find it so fascinating when I'm coming out of it, it's such an intense and unique kind of concentration. You realise how deeply you were in it, how completely focused you were on the act of writing. That level of concentration is sometimes difficult to sustain. At the same time it's extraordinary, because it's really necessary, it allows us to be truly in that moment of creation. So in the end, putting pen to paper is something that happens in various stages.

Éric Fottorino: Do you write several drafts, or do you focus on one sentence after another and not move on until you feel you've got it just right?

Leïla Slimani: I'll have an idea for a scene, I'll write it, then I'll leave it for a while, think about something else, start drafting another scene, then go back to it. I go back and forth. For example, I couldn't spend three weeks working on the same scene; I find it impossible because I get totally sick of it. So I often work on two or three scenes at the same time, two or three different ideas, then suddenly something will fall into place for one of them and I'll spend more time on that one, but I try not to get to the point where I'm fed up with my own book because that's really tough.

Éric Fottorino: Does the success you've had ever make you feel anxious or get in the way of writing your next book, or are you able to keep it all in perspective? Knowing you, and reading your work, I get the impression that you have a very healthy attitude towards success and that you're very clear-headed about carrying on with your writing.

Leïla Slimani: We've just come to the end of the big literary launch season, so my friends and I have been doing literary events, festivals, and so on. Some of them have worked for three or four years on huge books, incredible books, and after two or three weeks they've had their press officer telling them that their books aren't working, that it's not going to happen, that they haven't got on the prize longlists. To be honest, I'm never going to be one of those people who says, "I feel so much pressure, this is so hard", and so on. No, it's amazing. It's the greatest gift and the greatest privilege when you're a writer to be read by so many people, to enjoy good reviews and get a good reception. I want to embrace that happiness fully, on both a literary and a personal level. The pressure doesn't come from literary critics or from TV appearances, it comes from me. The thing I find difficult is to sit back down in front of my computer and write another novel. You can have all the prizes in the world, but no one will write the books for you. The moment you start writing is a moment of truth, one that's simultaneously terrifying and exhilarating. If you don't feel that fear, I don't see the point of writing.

Éric Fottorino: If you don't feel that fear ... right from the start?

On Writing

Leïla Slimani: It explains that chicken carcass ...

A member of the audience: Do you consider yourself a writer for life, or could you imagine one day saying: "I'm going to do something else. I've been a writer, I'm going to stop now and try something different"? Are there any other paths that tempt you even now? It's possible to do several things and not be a writer to the exclusion of all else.

Leïla Slimani: That's a very good question. I think I do consider myself a writer for life. That doesn't mean that I'll write in a routine way, that I'll bring out a book every two years, but I consider myself a writer for life in the sense that, first of all, I want to build a body of work: I'm curious to know what the future Leïla Slimani will find to write about, and so I want to go for it and see what happens. And then I think that sometimes writing is also about just making yourself do it. A lot of people think that you always do it gladly, but sometimes you do it unwillingly. You don't feel like it, you don't want to be alone, you don't want to spend your days staring at a blank page with no ideas coming. There's a kind of obligation, and I like that obligation, it keeps me going. And so I think I'll be a writer for life, but I hope that won't stop me doing plenty of other things. I'd like to learn judo ...

A member of the audience: I'm a choreographer, and so I've learnt dancing techniques, for all kinds of dances. I realised that I had a certain talent, but in order to tap into it I needed to learn the different techniques. Is a writing workshop the way you learn the techniques you need to become a writer? Is there anyone, apart from the greats, who could succeed without one?

Leïla Slimani: That's another very good question. And in fact there are conflicting views on this. In the United States, for example, it's all about technique. The writing workshop I enrolled in there was made up of six sessions over the course of six weeks. The sessions all took place in the evening, from 7 p.m. to 10 p.m., with a break in the middle for a drink or several – and so the second half was often much more relaxed than the first. It was much more the French style, laid-back and informal. In the United States, for example in Iowa or at Columbia, there are some writing courses that are very well known, because a lot of contemporary authors have graduated from them. So now those courses have come under fire, because several people think that in a way they're conditioning a certain kind of writer, resulting in a particular style of writing, and that now a whole generation of writers are producing the same kind of books. They have the technique, that's obvious. They're taught how to construct an opening, how to develop a plot, they're taught all sorts of things. In France, it's completely different. In France, writing courses are more like midwifery. They help you to give birth, in a way, to what you already know. And if you don't actually know it, if in reality you don't have either the desire or the discipline to write, or even, dare I say it, if you don't have a gift for writing, then they might tell you that they can't help you. They get you to write a few texts, and the workshop leader can see straight away who has understood, who's got it, and who hasn't. It's very hard to explain to someone that they haven't got it. It's not like dancing, where you can teach steps that the student can go away and practise. If a writer can't find within themselves a way to get close to their reader, if they can't find that indefinable essence of what turns a piece of writing into a novel, then it's almost impossible to explain it to them. And so no, in France there aren't as yet writing workshops that focus on technique in that way, not at all.

A member of the audience: Just now you mentioned that you can't spend three weeks writing a single scene, that it's too long for you, you stop and begin working on another one. You specifically used the word "scene". I wondered if, like Chekhov, you had also considered writing for the stage?

Leïla Slimani: Absolutely, and in fact I have written for the stage as part of the Paris des Femmes festival that took place at the Théâtre des Mathurins. It's a festival that showcases women writing for the stage, because very few women do that – I think that only twenty per cent of shows put on in Paris are written by women. So that was my first experience of theatrical writing. It was a very difficult writing form. The fact that you can only pass on information through the voice of the characters, through dialogue, and that you don't have that wonderful freedom that a novelist has – to describe, to digress, to offer flashbacks, to leave some things unsaid ... you no longer have that freedom. But it was a fantastic exercise and during the festival I was lucky enough to receive a grant from the National Centre for Cinema to extend my work on it, and write a longer play on the basis of the scene I had written.

Éric Fottorino: Can you talk to us a little about another of your books, *Sex and Lies: True Stories of Women's Intimate Lives in the Arab World*?[7] It's a research project that you carried out in North Africa, particularly in Morocco.

Leïla Slimani: Yes, it's a research project, but a literary one. When I went to launch my first book, *Adèle*, in Morocco, I did a tour of Moroccan cities. *Adèle* is a novel that deals with sexuality in quite a blunt way: it's about lies, hypocrisy and betrayal, and in every city I went to Moroccan women would come up to me and tell me about their sex lives, their private lives, the difficulties they face in a country where laws about sexuality are very harsh, very oppressive, but where, at the same time, the way of life in the big cities is increasingly similar to western ways of life. So these women were torn, very divided between two different ways of seeing the world, and I wanted to make their voices heard. I wrote some analytical chapters in that book, but above all it's a series of unfiltered interviews with Moroccan women, told in their own words, their expressions, their whispers even, their hesitations. It was also a way for me to speak to a certain part of Moroccan society that does not want to deal with this subject, and to the authorities, too. To say to them: "You can't say that you didn't know, you can't say that this doesn't exist. You can say that you don't like it, fine, let's talk about it, that's not a problem, you can

---

7 *Sexe et mensonges, la vie sexuelle au Maroc.* English translation by Sophie Lewis, Faber & Faber, 2020.

say that you're against it, but you can't say that it doesn't exist". Today we live in a world – whether it's Moroccan society or other North African societies – where people try to deny certain realities because they don't fit within the moral framework that they would like to impose. And yet today, there's a whole part of the reality of life, for young people in particular, that no longer fits within those frameworks that others would like to impose. That's what I wanted to discuss in *Sex and Lies*.

Éric Fottorino: A member of the audience has asked how you feed your imagination. I'm fascinated to know the answer to this, and we're going to bring this inspiring conversation to a close on that subject …

Leïla Slimani: My mother would tell you that it was already well fed when I was very young! I was born with an overactive imagination. I think that it's something in my nature, by which I mean that as a child I already had a very well-developed imagination, and a very strange relationship to reality. I didn't really distinguish between reality and fiction, and I found it very difficult when I was forced to do so – and the older I got, the more I was forced to do so. Otherwise, I feed it firstly by reading, which for me is the number one writing workshop. I also feed it by watching movies; I go to the cinema a lot. And then by observation, too: that's what led me to my career as a journalist and reporter. I think that learning to observe, to sit somewhere, saying nothing, just watching how people behave, how they walk, how they talk, how they hold an object, that's the magic of reporting. You might read an opening scene that tells you about a man in the street, selling vegetables in front of his house, and from the way he's presented you understand that he's living through a war, or a crisis, you understand that he's living in poverty because of tiny details. So I feed my imagination by observing, by reading and by watching films.

And by walking these streets, which hold the best stories of all.

My Heroine: Simone Veil

My Heroine: Simone Veil

Ever since I was a teenager, I've had a picture of Simone Veil hanging above my desk. In the photograph she has a white blouse, and is wearing her long black hair down. She's looking straight at the camera with an impressive determination. She's as beautiful as a film star. She was my hero.

Her autobiography, which confirmed her status as an important writer and which was a massive and well-deserved success, was simply titled *A Life*. As if her life were just one existence among others, banal and ordinary. And yet, what a life it was. For a long time I've thought that Simone Veil is like a character in a novel. Just like in the greatest works of literature, this incredibly beautiful and strong young woman had her childhood cruelly wrenched from her, caught up in the macabre whirlwind of history. The girl who turned sixteen at Birkenau, who experienced the horror of the death marches, became the first woman president of the European Parliament whose motto was "Never again". Just like in the novels, she met the love of her life and loved him till the day she died. And just like all legendary characters, she was impossible to pin down, forged of contradictions and silences. The nice little middle-class girl was also a rebellious adolescent, combative and reckless. The woman who was always pictured with her hair in a bun, wearing a suit, a pearl necklace and a pussybow blouse, is scandalous, wayward, insolent. What novelist would have dared to dream up such a noble heroine, one who would devote her life to defending orphans, prisoners, AIDS victims?

After the horror of the concentration camps, Simone Veil could well have been forgiven for wanting a comfortable life, filled with love and tenderness. But she chose political commitment: however fierce the debate was, she never walked away from it. She forced herself to confront the world head-on, and to refuse the comfort of middle-class indifference. In her famous address to the National Assembly in November 1974, as she was defending the law that would legalise the voluntary termination of pregnancy, she asked this fundamental question: "Why shouldn't we carry on looking the other way?" Every one of us has to ask ourself this question one day. How do we resist the temptation of silence and selfishness? How do we stop looking away? Can life have any sense if it is lived in deliberate ignorance of the suffering of others?

We need to open our eyes, and our ears, too. "All we need to do is listen to women" was the challenge she threw down to a parliament made up almost entirely of men. It seems like an obvious point. Yet she was a revolutionary, for she was brought up in a time when women were not allowed a voice. When girls were taught "you don't say that" and "you don't do that". When shame was as much to blame for their death as the mutilations inflicted on their bodies. Simone Veil forced everyone to open their eyes to an intolerable situation. She was born in a France that did not allow women the right to vote. She grew up in a country where wives had to ask their husband's permission to have a bank account, or to own a chequebook, a country where it was impossible to buy the pill. A France that hid away underage mothers, where fatherless children were called bastards. Where backstreet abortionists carried out their procedures in cellars, where women were maimed for life by these barbaric operations. She was born into a family where her own mother gave up work under pressure from Veil's father. She herself had to haggle with her husband just to be able to have a career. She would eventually become a magistrate, because her husband could not come to terms with her being a lawyer.

And yet even if she couldn't practise law, she changed the law for all women. She pleaded our cause with an exceptional rigour and political intelligence. Her feminism was pragmatic and her commitment to legalise abortion was also a class issue. "What's the point of a law that the upper classes can get around and the poorest die from?" she asked the members of parliament. There is still a large part of today's world that is like France was back then. In my country, Morocco, hundreds of clandestine abortions are carried out every day. Babies are found in dustbins. While the richest women go to Europe for an abortion, thousands of women with lesser means commit suicide or die from taking toxic substances. It is estimated that throughout the world, fifty thousand women die every year as a result of clandestine abortions. No one listens to those women. We act as if they didn't exist. Our honour is intact, that's all that matters!

Ever since Simone Veil died, thousands of women have expressed their gratitude towards her. Because thanks to her, French women no longer have to endure that humiliation. But her example should also oblige us not to look the other way, should forbid us from doing so. "Barbarity never dies", she said. It is always lying in wait, somewhere, and despite our fear, despite our cowardice, we have to believe that we can and must stand up and fight. With our eyes and hearts open, just as she taught us.

Selected Quotations from Simone Veil

"No woman seeks an abortion with lightness of heart.
All we need to do is listen to women.
This is an enduring tragedy".

26th November 1974, addressing the National Assembly

"[Women in politics]
should not be something to laugh or joke about".

22nd June 1996
Meeting of the national council of the UDF
(Union for French Democracy)

"The demand I make as a woman is that my difference be acknowledged, that I should not be obliged to adapt to a masculine model".

Episode 4 of *Contact: The Encyclopedia of Creation*
Canadian documentary programme hosted by Stéphan Bureau,
2006

"I am not a militant at heart,
but I am a feminist,
in solidarity with all women,
whoever they may be".

Interview with the newspaper *Libération*, 1995

"I have the distinct impression that,
on the day I die,
I will be thinking of the Shoah".

78651

Simone Veil's registration number at Auschwitz

"The danger is no longer that we do not speak of the Shoah, but that we speak of it unwisely".

During the commemoration of the raid on the
Winter Velodrome in Paris,
17th July 2005

"In the course of the twentieth century, Europe led the world into war twice.
Henceforth, Europe must stand for peace".

NEVER AGAIN!

"By setting itself grand ambitions, Europe can make its voice heard and stand for strong values:
peace, the defence of human rights, greater solidarity between the rich and the poor.
Europe is the grand design of the twenty-first century".

As the first female President of the European Parliament
(1979–1982)

"I still believe that it is always worth fighting for what we believe in.
And whatever anyone might say, humanity today is more bearable than it was in the past".

Interview with the newspaper *Libération*, 1995

"For as long as we listen to one another,
and share with one another,
we live as one".

Episode 4 of *Contact: The Encyclopedia of Creation*
Canadian documentary programme hosted by
Stéphan Bureau, 2006

"I am not one of those people who fear the future.
The younger generations sometimes surprise us in the
ways that they are different from us; we ourselves have
raised them differently from how we were raised.
But these young people are brave, just as capable of
passion and sacrifice as their parents and grandparents
before them.
We must learn to trust that they will hold onto the
supreme value of life".

26th November 1974,
addressing the National Assembly

"You know, despite everything I have lived through, I am an optimist, and I will always be an optimist. Life has taught me that over time, progress always wins. It is long, it is slow, but ultimately I have faith".

Interview with the newspaper *Libération*, 1995

Thank you

Simone Veil's last words before her death